Phoebe and the Spelling Bee

SCHOLASTIC INC.

New York   Toronto   London   Auckland   Sydney

ISBN 0-590-68958-4

Copyright © 1996 by Barney Saltzberg.
All rights reserved.
Published by Scholastic Inc., 555 Broadway, New York, NY 10012,
by arrangement with Hyperion Books for Children,
an imprint of Disney Book Publishing, Inc.
Nestlé is a registered trademark of Nestlé USA, Inc.

SCHOLASTIC and associated logos are trademarks and/or registered trademarks of
Scholastic Inc.

12 11 10 9 8 7 6 5 4 3 2 1   8 9/9 0 1 2 3/0

Printed in the U.S.A.   24

First Scholastic printing, October 1998

The artwork for each picture is prepared using ink and color wash.
This book is set in 17-point American Typewriter.

"Friday we will have our first spelling bee," announced Ms. Ravioli. "Here's a list of words you should know."

I slid down in my chair. "I'm going to be sick on Friday," I whispered to Katie.

"Don't be silly, Phoebe," said Katie. "Spelling is easy."

"I'm allergic to spelling," I told her.

"I'll help you," said Katie.

We ate lunch together. Katie looked over the spelling list. "This will be a breeze!" she said.

I drew dots all over my arm and started groaning, "Oooohhhh!"

"What's the matter?" asked Katie.

"I think I've got chicken pox!" I said.

"Spell **actor**," said Katie.

"**A-k-d-o-r**," I said.

"That's what it sounds like," said Katie, "but it's spelled differently."

She showed me the word on the spelling list. I saw that you could break the word into two parts—**act** and **or**.

"If I could **act or** spell, I'd **act**!" I said. "**A-c-t-o-r!**"

"That's right!" said Katie.

"Try spelling **brontosaurus**," said Katie.

I dropped to the ground, holding my leg. "Oh, it's broken!" I cried. "A **brontosaurus** knocked me over, and I broke my leg!"

"I'm waiting!" said Katie.
"Race you to class backward," I shouted,
and then I ran inside.

That night
Katie called me
to find out how
I was doing
with my spelling list.

"Great!" I said.

I was folding
the spelling list
into a paper
airplane.

The next morning Ms. Ravioli asked how many
students had been studying for the spelling bee.
Everyone raised their hand. Except me.
I was under the table, studying my shoes.

"Phoebe," said Ms. Ravioli, "have you looked at your spelling list?"

I sat up in my chair. "Once there was an **actor** who played a **brontosaurus**."

Everybody laughed. I sank in my chair.

"Settle down, class," said Ms. Ravioli. "It sounds like Phoebe has an unusual way of learning her words."

I looked at Katie's spelling list on our way home.
"Try spelling **graceful**," she said.
"The **actor** who played a **brontosaurus** was
graceful!" I said.

"You're great at making up stories," said Katie.
"But the spelling bee is in three days!"

"I know," I said. Then I ran to get some ice cream.

I knew I had better study or I would really embarrass myself at the spelling bee.

I found my spelling list on my bedroom floor, still folded into an airplane.

"If I can fly this into the trash can on the first try," I thought, "I'll be the winner of the spelling bee."

The plane flew under a chair. "That was just a warm-up."

The plane flew into the wall. "Didn't count."

I stood on a chair
and dropped the airplane
into the trash. "Yes!"

I had a victory celebration
and danced around my room.

Then my father told me
it was time to go to bed.

The next morning Ms. Ravioli said we would have a mock spelling bee.

I decided it was time to get sick.

"Ooooh!" I moaned.

"What seems to be the problem?" asked Ms. Ravioli.

"I ate too many pieces of pizza with pineapple last night," I said. "I feel sick."

"I think a visit to the nurse's office would be a good idea," said Ms. Ravioli.

"You haven't studied at all, have you?" whispered Katie.

"Yes I have!" I said.

I dragged my feet to the
nurse's office. Now my stomach
really did feel awful.

I had never lied to Katie before.

When I got back from the nurse's office, Katie
handed me a note. It said:

YOU DIDN'T STUDY AND YOU
DIDN'T HAVE A STOMACHACHE
AND REAL FRIENDS TELL EACH
OTHER THE TRUTH!

I didn't speak to Katie for the rest of the day.

That night I felt terrible. I hadn't been honest with my best friend, and I wasn't ready for the spelling bee.

I looked at my spelling list.

The first word I learned was **method**. I thought of a caveman saying his name, "**Me, Thod**."

I learned **telephone** by thinking of a phone, which you *tell* your friends things on. The second **l** in *tell* becomes an **e**.

I even learned how to spell **consonant**. It was easy because I figured there were three parts, **con**, **son**, and **ant**.

The next day was Friday. Spelling bee day.

I brought Katie a tulip and said I was sorry for having lied.

Ms. Ravioli explained the rules. I could feel my heart beating fast. What if I looked stupid in front of the whole class?

I started to raise my hand to go to the nurse's office. I decided to have the flu.

Katie wished me good luck. I was happy she was still talking to me. I put down my hand.

I decided not to have the flu after all.

During the spelling bee, Sheldon couldn't spell **disaster**. So he had to sit down.

When Jorge couldn't spell **telephone** correctly, he asked to go to the bathroom.

Marcia almost remembered how to spell **consonant**, but she forgot one of the **n**s.

I had to spell **Wednesday**. I knew the word had three parts, all with three letters.

I thought of a wedding day where chocolate chips were thrown instead of rice. **Wed** for wedding, **nes** for Nestlé chocolate, and **day**!

I spelled the word, "**W-e-d-n-e-s-d-a-y**."

"Nice job!" said Ms. Ravioli.

Katie spelled her word perfectly. **"N-a-t-u-r-a-l,"** she said.

After a while there were only three of us still spelling, and then came **brontosaurus**. I tried sounding it out, **"b-r-a-w-n-t-o-e-s-o-r-u-s."**

"That was a good try," said Ms. Ravioli, "but it's not the correct spelling."

"The **actor** was a **natural** and very **graceful**," I said. The whole class was staring at me.

"The **a-c-t-o-r** played a **brontosaurus** and met a caveman who said, '**Me, Thod**,' which is how you break down the spelling of **method**. Thod asked the dinosaur if he had heard about the volcano **disaster**. The dinosaur said no, but he wondered if Thod knew what a **c-o-n-s-o-n-a-n-t** was."

I looked at Ms. Ravioli.

"Please continue," she said.

So I did. "Thod and the dinosaur heard a **t-e-l-e-p-h-o-n-e** ringing in a tree!"

Katie smiled.

"The call was for a **p-e-d-e-s-t-r-i-a-n** who was jogging by, eating a piece of **c-h-o-c-o-l-a-t-e**."
I told my class that a great way to remember how to spell **chocolate** is to think of someone named *Choco*, who's *late*.

"When Choco saw the **brontosaurus**, he screamed and ran the other way! The caveman and the dinosaur fell on the ground and laughed!

"That's the **l-e-g-e-n-d** of Thod and the brontosaurus. You can remember how to spell **legend** by thinking of your **leg** and **end**!"

Everybody clapped when I finished. Even though I couldn't spell **brontosaurus**, I had used up all the words on my list to tell a story. Charlie couldn't spell **brontosaurus** either—but Katie could, so she won the spelling bee. She was great!

Ms. Ravioli gave Katie a certificate that said *CHAMPION SPELLER*.

I got a certificate, too, only mine said *WONDERFUL IMAGINATION!*